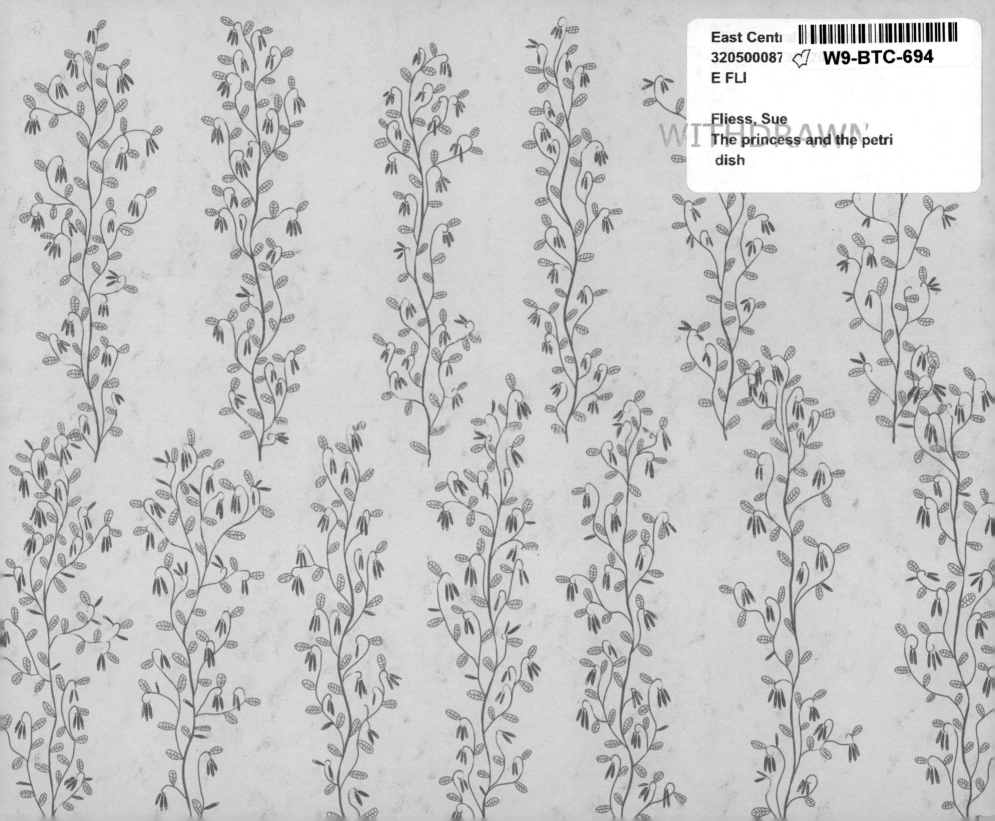

THE PRINCESS AND THE PETRI DISH

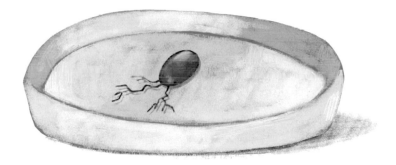

Sue Fliess   pictures by Petros Bouloubasis

Albert Whitman & Company
Chicago, Illinois

To Bobbi Weesen-Baer, for planting the seed—SF

To little "Cheddar"—PB

Library of Congress Cataloging-in-Publication data is on file with the publisher.

Text copyright © 2020 by Sue Fliess
Pictures copyright © 2020 by Albert Whitman & Company
Pictures by Petros Bouloubasis
First published in the United States of America in 2020 by Albert Whitman & Company
978-0-8075-6644-2 (hardcover)
978-0-8075-6645-9 (ebook)

Printed in China
10 9 8 7 6 5 4 3 2 1 WKT 24 23 22 21 20 19

Design by Rick DeMonico

For more information about Albert Whitman & Company,
visit our website at www.albertwhitman.com.

In a kingdom, long ago,
there lived a girl with dreams.
A princess and her petri dish
took science to extremes.

Princess Pippa questioned things.
She followed her own path.
While other girls were curtsying,
she brushed up on her math.

$5 \times A^2 : 1000 -$
$62 \times B^3 + 0.1 +$
000

Her parents built a lab for her
and filled it with supplies.
She wanted to make something great
or maybe win a prize.

Yet Pippa's lab experiments were never a success.

Her hand soap turned your fingers blue.

Her slime balls made a mess.

Her bubble gum was brittle.

Her fizzy soda, flat.
Her mouthwash made your breath smell bad...
and no one wanted that.

One evening during dinnertime,
the queen said, "Eat your peas."
But Pippa thought they tasted dull.
"Can I just skip them, please?"

When Pippa scooped them with her fork
and Mother looked away...
she slipped them in her pocket.
No, I won't eat peas today!

And that's when Pippa hatched a plan.
"I'll grow a better pea!
With flavor so delicious
all the people will agree!"

She grabbed a brand-new petri dish
and started right away.
She lined the dish with paper towels
and set it on a tray.

She took a pea and cocoa bean,
extracting cells with care,
then joined the two together.
"They'll make the sweetest pair!"

a)

b)

c)

💡#1

+

=

She watched and watered every day,
and soon it grew a root.
Then Pippa saw, to her delight,
it sprouted up a shoot!

Soon the pea outgrew the dish.
She moved it to a pot.
And when its size exceeded that,
she found a garden plot.

She opened up a pod with hope.
"It's time to check and see..."
She popped one in her mouth and said,
"The world's first chocolate pea!"

The peas became an instant hit
with kids and parents too.
The candymaker tried her peas
and gave a rave review!

The kingdom could not get enough
of Pippa's Chocolate Peas.
They sprinkled them on everything
from pancakes to grilled cheese!

Tending to her plants one day,
she noticed something wrong.

"These plants have grown too fast," she said.
"These vines are way too long."

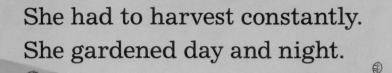

She had to harvest constantly.
She gardened day and night.

Poor Pippa hadn't slept in days.
And soon she lost the fight…

"Maybe just one nap," she yawned...
She slept a week instead!

Dreams of twisting, twirling pea vines swirled around her head.

When Pippa woke, to her surprise,
the plants were ten feet tall!

They covered half the countryside.
They'd breached the garden wall.

Pippa looked around her lab
and swiveled in her chair.
She checked her past experiments,
"The answer's here somewhere..."

Princess Pippa worked all night
to make the perfect mix.
And seeing the result, she said,
"I think I've found a fix!"

She spritzed the vines around her
with the mixture she'd created,
then hoped her math was accurate,
and held her breath and waited…

Soon the vines began to shrink.
"It's working!" Pippa cried.
"The plants are back to normal now.
The peas are safe inside."

The princess gave instructions
to the people of the town.
They showered pea vines left and right
and shrunk those pea plants down!

When the last plant had been tamed,
the kingdom breathed a sigh.
"Pippa's our best scientist!
A fact we can't deny!"

The princess and her petri dish
had proven dreams come true.
Then Princess Pippa shouted,
"Let's discover something new!"

💡 #2